MW01044959

First published 1985

Ashton Scholastic Limited
165 Marua Road, Panmure, P.O. Box 12328, Auckland 6, New Zealand.

Ashton Scholastic Pty Ltd
P.O. Box 579, Gosford, NSW 2250, Australia.

Scholastic Inc.
730 Broadway, New York NY 10003, USA.

Scholastic-TAB Publications Ltd
123 Newkirk Road, Richmond Hill, Ontario L4C 3G5, Canada.

Scholastic Publications Ltd
9 Parade, Leamington Spa, Warwickshire CV32 4DG, England.

National Library of New Zealand
Cataloguing-in-Publication data

FOX, Mem, 1946—
A cat called Kite/by Mem Fox; illustrated
by Kelvin Hawley. — Auckland, N.Z. : Ashton
Scholastic, 1985. — 1 v. — (Read by reading series)
Children's story.
ISBN 0-908643-38-1
428.6 (NZ823.2)
1. Readers (Elementary). I. Hawley, Kelvin.
II. Title. III. Series.

543 78/8

Typesetting by Rennies Illustrations
Printed in Hong Kong

A Cat Called Kite

by Mem Fox

illustrated by K·Hawley

EAD BY READING Series

Ashton Scholastic

uckland Sydney New York London Toronto

Once upon a time there was a cat called Kong...

WRONG!!

Once upon a time
there was a cat
called Kite...

RIGHT!

His teeth were long...

WRONG!!

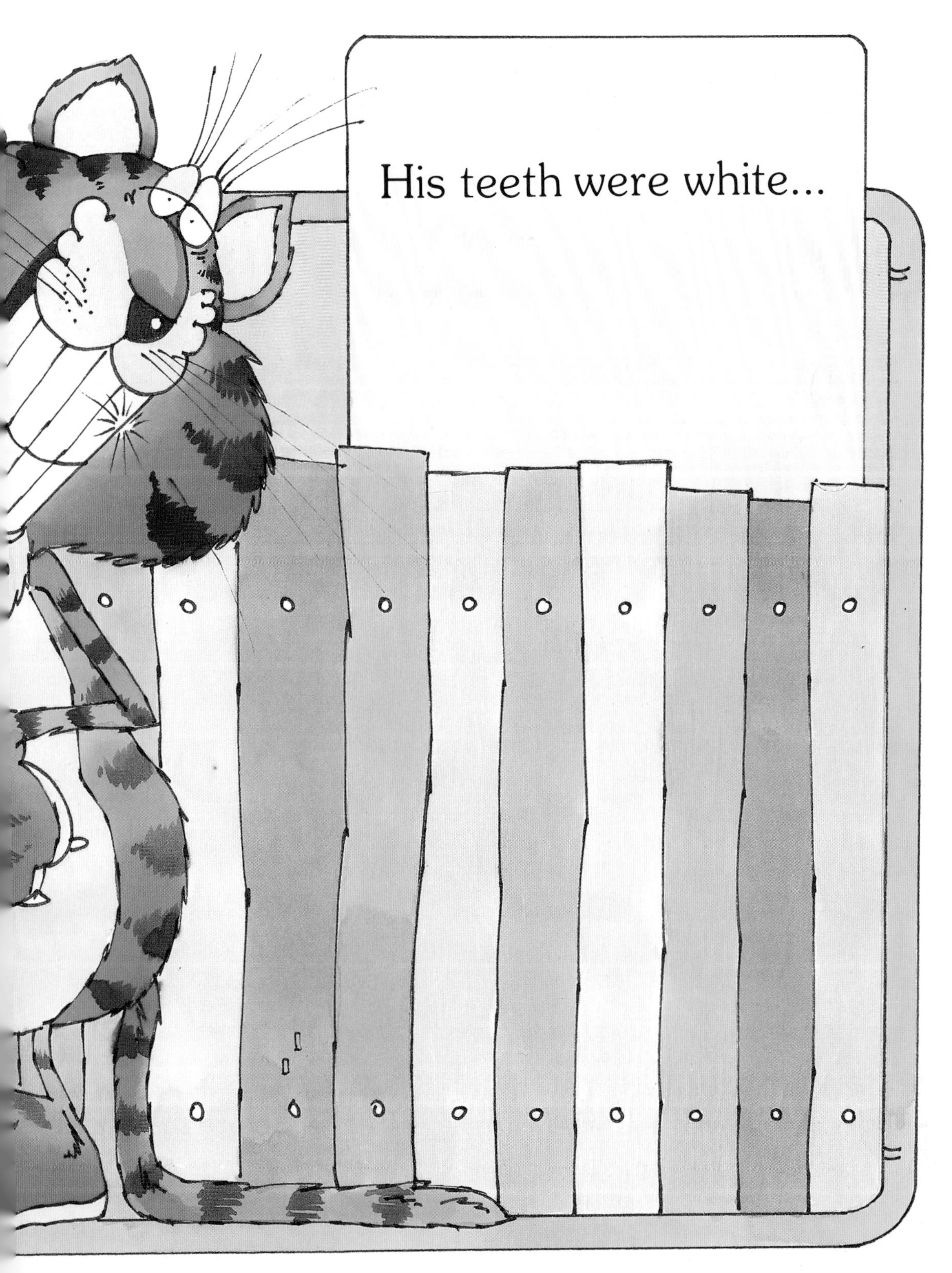
His teeth were white...

SAM
RIGHT!

His claws were strong...

SAM
WRONG!

He was scared
to fight...

RIGHT!

His eyes
were as round
as a Chinese gong...

WRONG!!
AM

His eyes
were as yellow
as the moon
at night...

SAM
RIGHT!

His lady love
was called Mee Long...

SAM
WRONG!

His lady love
was called Dee Lite...

RIGHT!

Early
one morning
he sang her
a song...

WRONG!

He sang her a song
in the dead of night...

RIGHT!

His lady love
adored that song...

WRONG!

His lady love
took off in fright...

RIGHT!

They married
each other
before too long...

WRONG!!

Kite stayed single
all his life,
and Dee became
another cat's wife.